THERE'S A NIGHTMARE IN MY CLOSET

written and illustrated by Mercer Mayer

Dial Books for Young Readers | *New York*

Published by Dial Books for Young Readers
A Division of Penguin Books USA Inc.
375 Hudson Street · New York, New York 10014
Copyright © 1968 by Mercer Mayer · All rights reserved
Library of Congress catalog card number: 68-15250 · Printed in the United States of America
ISBN: 0-8037-8682-4 · ISBN: 0-8037-8683-2 (lib.bdg.)

Marianna

From cotton to rabbit

There used to be a nightmare in my closet.

Before going to sleep,

I always closed the closet door.

I was even afraid to turn around and look.

When I was safe in bed, I'd peek...

sometimes.

One night I decided to get rid of my nightmare once and for all.

As soon as the room was dark, I heard
him creeping toward me.

Quickly I turned on the light and caught him
sitting at the foot of my bed.

"Go away, Nightmare, or I'll shoot you," I said.

I shot him anyway.

My nightmare began to cry.

I was mad…

but not too mad.

"Nightmare, be quiet or you'll wake
Mommy and Daddy," I said.

He wouldn't stop crying so I took
him by the hand

and tucked him in bed

and closed the closet door.

I suppose there's another nightmare in my closet, but my bed's not big enough for three.